from ancient India

ONCE
A MOUSE ...

a fable cut in wood

by MARCIA BROWN

ALADDIN PAPERBACKS

TO HILDA

First Aladdin Paperbacks edition 1982
Second Aladdin Paperbacks edition 1989

Copyright © 1961 by Marcia Brown

ALADDIN PAPERBACKS
An imprint of Simon & Schuster
Children's Publishing Division
1230 Avenue of the Americas
New York, New York 10020

Printed in Hong Kong

20 19 18 17 16 15 14 13

Library of Congress Cataloging-in-Publication Data
Brown, Marcia
Once a mouse.
Originally published in 1961 by Scribner.
Summary: As it changes from mouse to cat to dog to tiger,
a hermit's pet also becomes increasingly vain.
1. Fables. 2. Folklore—India.
1. Title.
PZ8,2.B668 on 1989   398.24'52   89-32057
ISBN 0-689-71343-6

One day a hermit
sat thinking about
big and little—
Suddenly,
he saw a mouse

about to be snatched up by a crow.

He hurried

to help the poor little animal, and tearing him
from the crow's greedy beak, he carried him off to

his hut in the forest, where he comforted him
with milk and grains of rice. But look!

A cat came to the hut with whiskers

straight and tail held high.

But the hermit was mighty at magic as well as at prayer. When he saw the danger threatening his little pet, he quickly changed him into a stout cat. But . . .

that night a dog barked in the forest.
Poor puss ran to hide under the bed. The
hermit wasted no time in thinking about
how big or so big, and

changed the cat into a big dog. Not long after that,
a hungry tiger

was prowling in the forest, and leaped on the
dog. Fortunately, the hermit was nearby,

and

with a gesture, he changed the dog

into a handsome, royal tiger. Now,

imagine the pride of that tiger! All day long he peacocked about the forest, lording it over the other animals.

The hermit missed nothing of all this, and chided the beast. "Without me," he would say to him, "you would be a wretched little mouse, that is, if you were still alive. There is no need to give yourself such airs."

The tiger felt offended and humiliated. He forgot all the good he had received from the old man.

"No one shall tell me that I was once a mouse.
I will kill him!"

But the hermit read the tiger's mind.
"You are ungrateful! Go back to the forest and
be a mouse again!"
So the proud and handsome tiger turned back
into a frightened, humble, little mouse,

that ran off into the forest and was never seen again. And the hermit sat thinking about big— and little . . .